TRACK THAT MONKEY!

Adapted by Casey Neumann

Based on the teleplay "Pups Save Big Hairy" by James Backshall and Jeff Sweeney

Illustrated by MJ Illustrations

A Random House PICTUREBACK® Book

Random House 🏠 New York

© 2019 Spin Master PAW Productions Inc. All rights reserved. Published in the United States by Random House Children's Books, a division of Penguin Random House LLC, 1745 Broadway, New York, NY 10019, and in Canada by Penguin Random House Canada Limited, Toronto. Pictureback, Random House, and the Random House colophon are registered trademarks of Penguin Random House LLC. PAW Patrol and all related titles, logos, and characters are trademarks of Spin Master Ltd. Nickelodeon, Nick Jr., and all related titles and logos are trademarks of Viacom International Inc.

rhcbooks.com

ISBN 978-0-525-64748-5

Printed in the United States of America

10 9 8 7 6 5 4 3 2 1

One day, the PAW Patrol were in the jungle helping their friends Carlos and Tracker give the monkeys their yearly checkups. Tracker used his magnifying glass to examine Mandy the monkey. "I'm ready to take Mandy's X-ray!" said Marshall.

Mandy put her face behind Marshall's scanner. The image of her bones surprised the other monkeys, and they started running in circles. "Uh-oh! How do we calm them down?" asked Rocky. "Scratch their backs!" said Carlos. "Monkeys love that!"

Rocky extended the claw from his Pup Pack and went to work scratching backs. The monkeys quickly relaxed.

"Looks like you've made some new friends, Rocky!" Marshall yelped.

Just then, a giant monkey named Big Hairy peeked around the rock he was hiding behind and saw Rocky's back scratcher. He really wanted to have his back scratched!

Chase and Zuma arrived, back from searching the jungle.

"We looked all over, but we didn't find any more monkeys who need a checkup," said Chase.

Carlos decided it was time to close the monkey checkup center. He thanked the PAW Patrol for their help.

Marshall invited Tracker to come back with the pups for a visit.
The pups happily scampered into the PAW Patroller as Carlos
and the monkeys waved goodbye.

The PAW Patroller rumbled along the jungle road. Suddenly, big bunches of bananas landed on the roof.

"*¿Escucharon?*" Tracker asked. "Did anyone else hear that?"

Ryder and the pups didn't see anything outside.

"Probably just some bumps in the road," Ryder suggested. They didn't realize that Big Hairy was riding on the roof of their vehicle!

As the PAW Patroller rolled into town, Big Hairy saw the giant cup on top of Mr. Porter's lemonade stand. He leaped from the vehicle onto the stand's roof. He rubbed his back against the huge cup—and it broke loose and crashed to the ground!

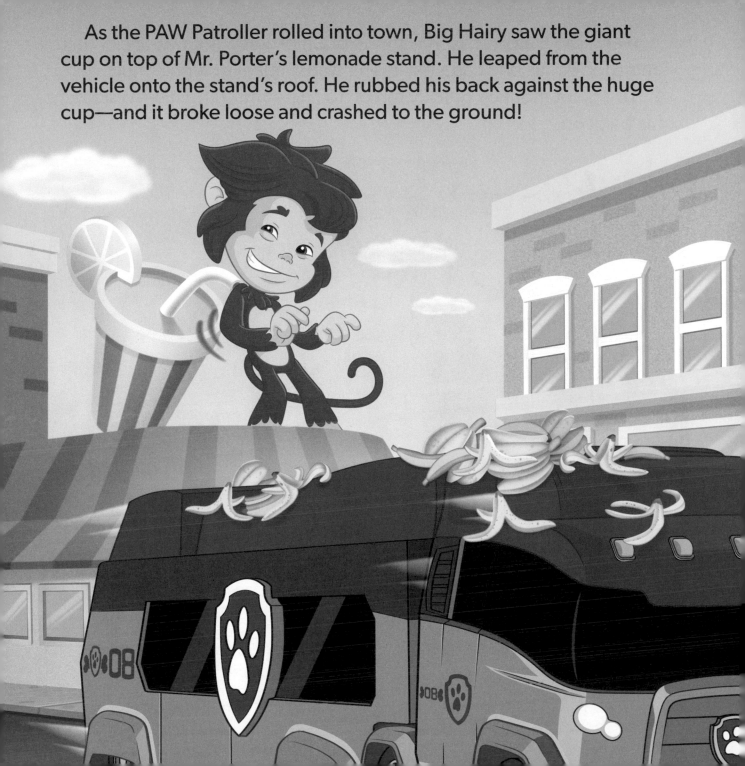

Next, Big Hairy ran to the statue of Chickaletta in front of city hall and rubbed his back against it. The statue fell over with a thud!

The giant monkey quickly ran off to find something else to scratch his back on.

Mayor Goodway discovered the statue of Chickaletta lying on the sidewalk.

"How did this happen?" she cried. Then she heard the sound of bells ringing and looked up. She couldn't believe her eyes—a giant monkey was shaking the bell tower on top of city hall!

Mayor Goodway immediately called the PAW Patrol.

Ryder gathered the pups at the Lookout and told them about Big Hairy.
"We'd better get him home before he causes any more monkey trouble!" he said.

For this mission, Ryder needed Rocky's big claw and catapult. He also needed Tracker's jeep and his super hearing.

"Green means go!" shouted Rocky.

"I'm all ears!" Tracker exclaimed. *"¡Todos oídos!"*

"The PAW Patrol is on the roll!" Ryder said. He and the two pups rushed to their vehicles.

The team found Big Hairy outside Mr. Porter's market. Rocky used his catapult to launch bananas at the monkey. Tracker tried to lure him away by pulling the banana-filled wagon with his cables.

The giant monkey wasn't interested.

"Why isn't he going after the bananas?" Rocky asked.

That was when Ryder noticed that Big Hairy was scratching his fur and pointing at Rocky's claw.

"He wants his back scratched with the best back scratcher ever, like the other monkeys did!" said Ryder. Just then, Big Hairy grabbed Rocky and took off! "After that giant monkey!" shouted Ryder.

Ryder called the rest of the PAW Patrol together. They chased Big Hairy and surrounded him on a bridge.

"Big Hairy, please let Rocky go!" begged Ryder.

But Big Hairy didn't want to. He turned and leaped off the bridge!

Big Hairy landed safely on the deck of Cap'n Turbot's boat, the *Flounder*.

"Sizzling sea serpents—I've never seen such a super-sized simian!" Cap'n Turbot exclaimed. "I need to shoot a series of snaps!"

He reached for his camera, but before he could get a shot, Big Hairy was gone!

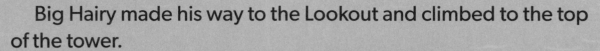

Big Hairy made his way to the Lookout and climbed to the top
of the tower.

Chase used his megaphone to check on Rocky.

"How are you doing up there, Rocky?" he called.

"I'm okay," Rocky replied. "But I'm getting tired of scratching!"

After a moment, Ryder had an idea!

Skye swooped in and nudged Big Hairy away from the edge of the roof. Then Zuma moved the periscope up and down from the control room to scratch Big Hairy's back.

He was so relaxed, he let go of Rocky.

Tracker used his cables as a zip line to bring Rocky down safely.
"Great work, Tracker!" said Ryder.

Skye dangled a bunch of bananas just out of Big Hairy's reach, then slowly lowered them to the roof. The giant monkey climbed down the Lookout and followed Skye to the PAW Patroller. Everything was back to normal . . . except Big Hairy's back was still itchy!

Rocky ran over to Big Hairy and gave him a giant back scratcher. "I made you something to remember me by!" Rocky exclaimed. Big Hairy was thrilled. He grabbed his new back scratcher and hopped onto the roof of the PAW Patroller. He was ready to head back to the jungle!

Ryder asked Robo Dog to take Big Hairy home, and soon the PAW Patroller began to roll away. Everyone said goodbye to the big monkey.

"And remember," Ryder called, "whenever you have an itch, just *ooka-ooka* for help!"

The pups laughed and cheered.